A Ch  of ♥ Heart

by Kristi McGee
illustrated by Linda Pierce

ⓖHarcourt

SCHOOL PUBLISHERS

Printed in China

ISBN 10: 0-15-350553-2
ISBN 13: 978-0-15-350553-9

Ordering Options
ISBN 10: 0-15-350335-1 (Grade 5 Below-Level Collection)
ISBN 13: 978-0-15-350335-1 (Grade 5 Below-Level Collection)
ISBN 10: 0-15-357552-2 (package of 5)
ISBN 13: 978-0-15-357552-5 (package of 5)

5 6 7 8 9 10   468   12 11 10 09

Josie screamed and ran. Her feet barely touched the ground. She didn't stop until she reached home. She and her friends were playing catch in the school yard when the ball flew by her and landed in Mrs. Freeman's yard next door. Josie opened the gate to Mrs. Freeman's yard. She took a step in. Then the front door opened. Mrs. Freeman's head popped out. Josie didn't hear what Mrs. Freeman said because she was too busy screaming and running away. If Mrs. Freeman caught her on her property, Josie didn't know what would happen. It wouldn't be good, according to what other kids said.

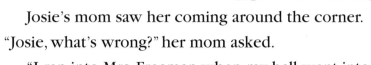

Josie's mom saw her coming around the corner. "Josie, what's wrong?" her mom asked.

"I ran into Mrs. Freeman when my ball went into her yard," she said.

Her mom frowned. "There's no need for you to fear Mrs. Freeman, Josie. Just because she keeps to herself doesn't mean you have to be afraid of her. I often chat with her at the market. She's a nice lady. She's never done anything to harm you. Has she?"

Josie had to admit her mom was right. Josie had never even spoken to Mrs. Freeman. Josie promised never to bother Mrs. Freeman again. She was still afraid, though. She had heard the rumors.

After dinner, Josie told her mom and dad about her school project. She was going to learn about a local hero in her town. Josie's teacher assigned Josie to research Mandy Johnson. She had been a nurse during World War II.

Josie's dad proposed a trip to the local library. They would go on Saturday. He would help her find information about the woman. Josie also wanted to find out about the jobs nurses did. She could hardly wait. She loved the library. She also loved spending time with her dad.

Saturday came and, with it, a trip to the library. Josie learned that Mandy Johnson had been an army nurse. She was stationed in North Africa. She also traveled all over Europe. She even received a Silver Star for showing "courage under fire." Josie couldn't believe it. What a brave lady!

Josie gave a full report to her class on Monday. She told her teacher and the class about Mandy Johnson. She told them where she served. She told them about her award.

Josie's teacher asked, "Did you find out if she is still living? Maybe you could interview her." Josie hadn't even thought of that. That would be great! She could meet a real hero!

The next week, Josie's father took her to the county courthouse. They looked at the public records.

"It says here that Mandy Johnson married Charles Freeman in 1945," Josie said. "They had a baby boy in 1947. Charles died in 1975. It looks like she is still alive. There's no record of her death."

Her dad said, "Let's look in the phone book." Josie opened it up and saw that were at least twenty Freemans listed in their community. "Well, it won't hurt to call a few and ask for Mandy Johnson," Josie's dad said.

That afternoon, Josie started making phone calls. She thought she would never find Mandy Johnson. She said over and over, "I'm sorry to bother you. I am looking for Mandy Johnson. She was a nurse during World War II."

Josie was ready to give up. Then she called the last person on her list, and she heard, "Why do you want to find her?" The woman on the phone sounded baffled. Josie explained about her class project. She told the woman how impressed she was with Miss Johnson. There was silence on the line.

"Well, you can come on over if you want. I'm Mandy Johnson. I'll answer your questions," the voice said.

"I've found her!" Josie mouthed to her father. "When can I come over?" asked Josie. Mandy Johnson said tomorrow afternoon. "Where do you live?" Then the look of excitement on Josie's face was replaced by a look of horror. It seemed that Mandy Johnson was the Mrs. Freeman all the kids were afraid of! However, Josie couldn't back out now. "I will see you tomorrow, Mrs. Freeman," Josie said.

The next afternoon, Josie and her mom walked to Mrs. Freeman's gate. "Go on," her mom said. "It will be fine."

Josie's stomach hurt. She was scared. She went up to the porch. Her foot hit the first step. Mrs. Freeman opened the door. Every instinct told Josie to run. Then Mrs. Freeman said, "Are you coming in or not?"

Josie climbed the stairs and went in, but she was still tempted to flee. Mrs. Freeman waved to Josie's Mom. "Th-th-thank you, Mrs. Freeman," Josie stuttered. She was relieved that Mrs. Freeman didn't seem to remember her.

Mrs. Freeman led Josie into the living room. A tray of cookies sat on the table. "Would you like some milk?" Mrs. Freeman asked. Josie nodded. She looked around. Everywhere she looked, she saw pictures of a handsome young man wearing a uniform. Mrs. Freeman returned and handed Josie her milk.

"Have a cookie, dear," said Mrs. Freeman. "What is it you want to know?"

Without even thinking, Josie said, "Who's that?" She pointed to the pictures.

"That's my son," said Mrs. Freeman.

"Where is he now?" Josie asked.

"He died in 1969. He was a soldier in the army," said Mrs. Freeman. For the first time, Josie realized Mrs. Freeman was not mean at all. She was only sad.

"I'm sorry," said Josie.

"Nothing for you to be sorry for," Mrs. Freeman replied. "Now about my story . . ."

Mrs. Freeman relayed the essence of her story. She told Josie all about being a nurse. She told her about helping soldiers during World War II. She told her how scared she had been during the German bombings, and how she had just kept doing her job. That was why she received the Silver Star award. She even showed Josie the medal. Josie could not believe it! Mrs. Freeman was such an interesting person, and she was nice, too! Not only that, she also seemed to like Josie's company.

When the interview was over, Mrs. Freeman said, "I suppose I won't be hearing from you again." She sounded sad.

"Actually, I live down the street," said Josie. "Can I stop by again?" Josie really liked Mrs. Freeman.

"I'd love the company. Come by anytime, dear," Mrs. Freeman replied with a smile.

The next week, Josie shared her report at school. She told about Mrs. Freeman's work. She told about seeing her medal. She even told about her son. The class wanted to hear more. Josie said she had learned something very important from the insights Mrs. Freeman shared.

"What I learned was not to judge people whom I don't know. Mandy Johnson is actually Mrs. Freeman. You know—the one who lives next to the school. When I met her, she gave no indication to make me afraid. She is a nice lady—she's just lonely. I spent the afternoon at her house, and she's not one bit scary. I am going back to visit tomorrow," Josie said with a smile. "I owe her a big apology."

"I think we can all learn a lesson from Josie's project," said Josie's teacher, and the rest of the class agreed.

Think Critically

1. Why did Josie scream and run at the beginning of the story?

2. How would you describe Mrs. Freeman?

3. What do phrases such as *after dinner*, *on Monday*, and *the next week* tell you about how the story is organized?

4. Is *A Change of Heart* a good title for the story? Why or why not?

5. Would you have acted the same way that Josie did? Why or why not?

 **Language Arts**

Write a Journal Entry Imagine that you are Josie. Write a journal entry that explains your change of heart from the beginning of the story to the end. Write about what you plan to say to Mrs. Freeman the next time you visit.

School-Home Connection Tell a family member about this story. Then discuss a change of heart you have had. Ask your family member whether he or she has ever had a change of heart.

Word Count: 1,224